Monsters and Magic

Tales of Ancient Greece

by

Joe Coleman

Watermill Press

Contents

Monster in the Maze

On the island of Crete, King Minos keeps a monster in a maze. The monster is like a man from the waist up, but from the waist down he has the body of a bull. The monster is called the Minotaur.

The Minotaur lives in such a confusing maze that no one has ever found the way out. Minos even killed the workers who built it so that the maze's secret would be safe.

Because the city of Athens has lost a war against King Minos, Minos demands that the Athenians send him fourteen hostages—the fairest youths and maidens—every nine years. When they arrive, Minos sends them into the maze of the Minotaur. There, one by one, the monster tracks them down and eats them.

But one year, the King of Athens sends his own son, Theseus. Theseus is the strongest and cleverest youth in all of Athens. He begs his father to let him go as one of the fourteen hostages.

"Impossible!" his father says.

"But I know I can kill the Minotaur!" says Theseus.

"Well, even if you do," says his father, "how will you get out of the maze? No one has ever escaped!"

"I'll find a way!" Theseus says.

So Theseus and the other thirteen hostages board a ship bound for the kingdom of Minos. Since death awaits them in the maze, the boat's sail is black.

Theseus's father makes one last request. "Son, if you kill the Minotaur, and if you get out of the maze alive, fly a *white* sail on the boat when you return."

Theseus promises, and the doomed men and women set sail for the kingdom of Minos.

As the hostages arrive, one person takes a special interest in Theseus — Ariadne, Minos's daughter. When Ariadne sees brave Theseus, she falls in

*Theseus boarded a ship bound for the
kingdom of Minos.*

love with him.

I must help him! she thinks to herself. And while no one is looking, she sneaks out of the palace and creeps down to the prison where the hostages are kept. At last, she finds Theseus.

Theseus sees the beautiful woman calling to him through the bars of his cell. He remembers that this is the king's daughter, for he has seen her standing beside Minos's throne.

They whisper together for a long time, and at last they come up with a plan. Theseus kisses Ariadne good-bye, and she sneaks back into the palace.

The next morning, guards march the fourteen hostages to the maze. Among them is Theseus, who hides a spool of thread given to him by Ariadne. As they stand at the door of the maze, they hear the horrible roar of the Minotaur from deep within the twisted halls.

"He's hungry!" laughs Minos. The hostages shudder.

The guards herd the Athenians into the maze. Once inside, Theseus quickly ties one end of the string to a rock near the entrance. He tells his fellow hostages to wait and, unwinding the string as he goes, he feels his way farther into the maze.

The air is cold in the dark, winding halls. Water drips from above. A terrible odor clings to the walls—the breath of the man-eating Minotaur. Theseus shudders as he creeps deeper into the maze.

Now, Theseus can hear the Minotaur. He strains his eyes at the darkness, trying to catch a glimpse of the monster.

Then a cold hand grabs him. Pain

shoots through his body. The grip is like steel. He turns to face the horrible creature itself. It has two long, pointed horns growing out of black curly hair, and its eyes are red. With its giant arms and chest, the top half of the Minotaur is twice the size of a man. From the waist down, it's all bull, a ferocious beast pawing the ground with jagged hooves.

The Minotaur eyes Theseus hungrily. "Minos feeds me well!" the Minotaur roars.

Theseus can't believe it! The Minotaur can speak! "I'm glad to see you," hisses the Minotaur. "I'm starved."

The stench of the monster's breath and the pain of its steely grip almost overwhelm Theseus. He struggles to get free as the Minotaur laughs.

"Minos feeds me well!" the Minotaur roared.

But Theseus is as clever as he is strong. He knows that he has to do something fast or he'll become food for this hideous beast. He has to use his wits.

Then Theseus has an idea. He pretends to faint.

For one split second, the Minotaur loosens its grip. That's all Theseus needs. At once, he springs into action. He spins around, leaps high into the air, and lands on the Minotaur's back. Without a weapon, Theseus has to rely on his own strength. He brings his fist crashing down on the Minotaur's head. The monster howls in pain.

It begins to run through the maze. Theseus hangs on with all his might. But the Minotaur is too strong. Theseus crashes onto the hard floor and is stunned by the fall. The Minotaur raises its front feet to trample him.

Theseus sees the jagged hooves poised over him. With his last bit of strength, he delivers a double blow to the monster's chest. It works. As the Minotaur bellows in pain, Theseus staggers to his feet. He knows he has to finish the job while the Minotaur is still stunned. Once more, he climbs onto the Minotaur's back. He grabs the large, powerful horns and puts his feet squarely on the monster's neck. Then he pulls back sharply on the horns.

The Minotaur bellows so loudly that the very earth shakes. Then, at last, Theseus hears a mighty *craaaack!* He has broken the monster's neck. The Minotaur kicks its legs and falls thrashing to the ground.

Theseus crawls out of the way of the dying monster and watches the Minotaur's slow death. Finally, all is quiet. The Minotaur is dead.

Theseus gropes in the dark for the thread. Slowly, he walks out, winding the thread back to the door of the maze. At last, he sees daylight. When he turns the last corner, he sees his fellow Athenians.

Rejoicing together, they walk out of the maze into the sweet light of day. Minos and the guards have gone, certain that all inside the maze would die. Only one person has waited behind — Ariadne.

When she sees Theseus, she smiles. "Theseus, my brave Theseus. I knew that you could kill the Minotaur."

Ariadne, Theseus, and the Athenians

15

"I knew that you could kill the Minotaur,"
Ariadne smiled.

rush to the shore to their waiting boat. Silently, they slip out to sea, leaving the land of Minos and the Minotaur behind.

At last, free from the horrible Minotaur, Theseus falls fast asleep. He has done well, except for one thing. He has forgotten the promise he made to his father. He has forgotten to raise the white sail.

The next morning, Theseus awakes, safely back at Athens. He expects to hear cheers and shouts. But the beach is deserted, and from the town, he can hear the sound of people crying and moaning.

What's wrong? he wonders as he gazes about him. Then, he looks at the sail and remembers. It's the black sail! He forgot to fly the white sail as his father had asked!

An old woman appears on the beach. Theseus calls to her, "All the hostages live. I killed the Minotaur!"

"Theseus! Is that you?" the old woman cries. At first, her face is happy. Then her eyes fill with tears.

"What is it?" asks Theseus.

"It's the king, your father. Every day and night since you left, he walked up and down the beach, looking for a sail — a white sail or a black sail. Last night, he saw your boat. Then he saw the saddest sight of his life — the black sail. He thought you were dead, Theseus, and it broke his heart. He jumped from these cliffs to the rocks below. Your father is dead, Theseus."

And so it was that, on the saddest day of his life, Theseus became king of Athens. He had killed the Minotaur and saved the youth of Athens from Minos. But because of one forgetful moment, his father was dead. The day that Theseus was crowned king was a day of joy mixed with sorrow.

Spiderwoman

It was a sunny winter day. Arachne
moved her wooden loom nearer the window and sat down to her weaving.
Arachne loved to weave. She loved the
steady movement of the shuttle and the
soft feel of the wool. Most of all, she loved
the brightly colored threads. On her
loom, she spun threads of red, green,
purple, and white, and some which shone

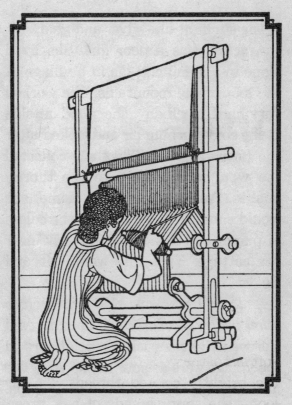

Arachne sat down to her weaving.

in the sunlight like silver and gold.

Arachne was a poor girl. She lived alone in a small cottage in a village at the foot of the mountains. She worked very hard. Each day, she stood outside in the cold morning air and looked after the farmers' sheep. Then she collected the wool which clung to the thorny bushes. And when she got home, she would spin it and dye it with the colors of plants and flowers which grew near her cottage. Then she would sit and weave.

At least I have one skill which gives other people pleasure, she thought. And she was right. Arachne's neighbors in the village were as poor as she was. The harsh winter had destroyed their crops. Many of them were hungry. But Arachne had woven their children warm woolen scarves and hats, so at least they were not cold. They loved Arachne for her kindness, and they loved the brightly colored clothes.

But there was someone who did not love Arachne or the clothes she made. That was the goddess Athena. Athena lived high up in the snow-peaked mountains that surrounded Arachne's village. Athena was also a weaver. And she believed that the cloth she wove was the most beautiful in the world. Because Athena was a goddess, her threads *were* silver and gold. And while Arachne could only make small items like hats and scarves, Athena wove flowing gowns and blankets.

One day, something bright caught Athena's eye. As she looked upon the village, she saw a woven red and yellow scarf wrapped snugly around a child's neck. The scarf glittered in the winter sun. It was beautiful. Athena decided to investigate.

She wore an old coat over her fine clothes and came down to the village. Looking through a window, she saw Arachne sitting at her loom, weaving. By Arachne's side lay a pile of brightly colored threads. She was humming to herself as she worked, and looked happy and content.

Suddenly, Athena grew jealous. Was it Arachne's contented face that made her feel this way? Or was it her beautiful, neat work? Whatever the reason, Athena was furious. Without knocking, she walked into the small cottage.

Arachne looked up at her visitor. "Hello," she said, smiling. "Would you like to look at my weaving?"

Athena felt her anger rising. She threw off her old coat and stood before Arachne in her finery.

"I am the goddess Athena," she snapped. "And I am the best weaver in the world. Why should I want to look at your careless work?"

Arachne was shocked. She did not know why this stranger was so angry, or so rude. "Madam," she replied politely. "You may be a fine weaver, but my work is not careless. I take great trouble to make everything I weave as perfect as possible. Why are you so unkind?"

Athena did not reply. As she stepped nearer to look at Arachne's work, she saw that it truly was perfect. Athena's jealousy grew stronger still.

"You must treat me with respect," she

demanded. "I am a goddess, and you must not answer back. If you truly believe your work is good, then prove it. We will have a contest. We will both weave a blanket. Then we shall see whose work is better."

Arachne was afraid. She did not want to compete with a goddess. And she could barely find enough wool to make a blanket.

"Be ready tomorrow morning," Athena said. "I shall return. Then we shall see who weaves better."

That night, Arachne could not sleep. She went to the mountainside and gathered all the wool she could find. When dawn came, she was still spinning.

As the sun rose over the mountain, Athena appeared at her door once again. "I have no time to waste," the goddess

"I have no time to waste," Athena said.
"Let us start at once."

said. "Let us start at once."

The two women sat on opposite sides of the room. Arachne's threads were the colors of a rainbow and shone brightly beside her. But Athena's were brighter. They sparkled like jewels in the morning sun.

All through the day, the women worked. They did not speak, and they hardly looked up from their looms. As evening drew near, the villagers came home from work. They walked past Arachne's cottage and peered through the window.

"That is the goddess Athena!" they whispered. "What is she doing with our neighbor Arachne?"

They gathered in front of the window and saw two beautiful blankets flowing from the looms. The light was fading but Arachne and Athena kept working. A few villagers went home to light their fires. But many stayed on. They wanted to support their kind friend.

Athena sensed this. It made her angry. *I'll show them I don't need their support,* she thought. *I'm a goddess, and they are mere humans.* The weavers continued in silence.

Finally Athena stopped. "I have finished," she cried triumphantly. "Look at my beautiful work!"

It was indeed beautiful. The silver and gold threads shimmered through the dazzling material. Not a stitch was out of place. It was a blanket fit for the gods.

The villagers stared through the window in silent admiration. "It is beautiful," they whispered to each other. But they did not dare to say it out loud. They were frightened of the goddess.

Then Arachne stopped weaving. She held up her blanket. It, too, was lovely, with colors as bright as a rainbow. The villagers cheered. "Beautiful, Arachne," they cried. "How clever you are. What a wonderful blanket you have woven."

The villagers' reaction made Athena even angrier than before. "Have you no judgment?" she screamed. "Why do you cheer for Arachne's work when you do not make a sound for mine?"

The villagers shrank back from the window in fear, and disappeared into the darkness. But Athena did not stop shouting. Arachne was terribly afraid.

"You and the villagers have made a fool of me," the goddess shouted. "I do not enjoy feeling like a fool." And with that, she picked up Arachne's blanket in one hand and a knife in the other. With a single movement, she cut the blanket in two.

After all her hard work, this was more than Arachne could bear. "Stop it," she cried. "Why are you doing this?"

The more Arachne cried, the more Athena cut. "This will teach you," she shouted. "Silly girl. You must learn never to compete with the gods."

But Arachne could not bear to watch as Athena tore her beautiful blanket to pieces. She ran to stop Athena. The goddess grabbed Arachne's hands and stopped her. Athena's fury was now out of control. She picked up Arachne's shuttle and broke it over the loom with such force that the loom collapsed in pieces. Arachne cried out in horror.

*Arachne cried out in horror as the loom
collapsed in pieces.*

"Cry all you like," Athena said. "You have nothing left. I have broken your loom and ruined your blanket." And with a cruel laugh, Athena stormed out of the door and was gone.

Alone and trembling, Arachne looked at the remains of her blanket. *All that work,* she thought miserably. *Now I have no wool left. If I cannot weave anymore, then there is no pleasure left in my life.*

With a heavy heart, she took the last remaining strands of wool and wove them into a noose. Then she put the noose around her neck and hanged herself.

Early the next morning, some villagers passed by Arachne's cottage. They were curious and peeked inside. To their horror, they saw Arachne's body hanging limply above the shredded remains of her beautiful blanket.

"Oh, Athena," they cried, raising their eyes to the snowy mountain top. "Why did you do this? Arachne was a kind girl who never harmed anyone."

Athena, warm under her shimmering new blanket, heard the villagers' cries. Suddenly, she realized that Arachne had killed herself. Her temper was over now. And she was shocked to think she had caused Arachne's death.

Athena returned to the village. In Arachne's cottage, she found the girl's body laid out on the bed. Athena felt deeply sorry. *I was jealous of Arachne,* she said to herself. *I was afraid her weaving was better than mine. And I was jealous of the villagers' love for her. But I did not want her to die.*

So, from the folds of her radiant gown,

Athena brought out a tiny glass bottle. In the light, its liquid reflected the colors of the rainbow—the colors of Arachne's weaving.

Athena sprinkled a few drops onto Arachne's still body. As she did, she spoke to her. "I cannot let you return as Arachne," she said. "Yet, you *shall* return to weave your colors and brighten the world."

When Athena left, all was quiet again in the little cottage. All was quiet, that is, except for the faint sound of a spider, spinning a delicate web. The web glistened like a rainbow in the bright sunlight.

World
of the Dead

One bright spring morning, a young girl named Persephone strolled through the fields, picking flowers.

Persephone was the daughter of the goddess Demeter. Demeter kept the fields rich with wheat and the vines heavy with fruit. Thanks to Demeter,

Hades was the driver of the chariot.

men and women were never hungry. Humans loved the goddess Demeter.

But people lived in fear of Hades, the god who ruled the world of the dead. Once a man passed into the world of the dead, he never returned.

Hades longed for a bride. As Persephone gathered flowers on this bright spring day, Hades decided that she would be his queen. As Persephone wandered through the fields, the sky suddenly grew dark. The earth rumbled and instantly split open.

Persephone stared in wonder as two mighty horses surged out of the earth. They breathed fire and tore the ground with their hooves. They pulled a chariot of gold from the earth. Persephone gasped. Hades was the driver! Without even leaving his chariot, Hades scooped

Persephone into his arms. Her cries were useless against the powerful god.

Hades held Persephone tightly against him with one arm. With the other, he guided his mighty beasts back to the underworld. Hades had claimed his bride.

Leaving the world of light behind her, Persephone now roamed the dark halls of death. Day and night, she wept. Her grief was so great that she refused to eat.

But someone heard Persephone's cries—her mother, Demeter. Demeter followed her daughter's voice but could find no trace of her. She searched the forests, the towns, the mighty seas. No one knew what had become of Persephone.

At last, in despair, Demeter asked the Sun. No one could hide from the all-seeing Sun. Demeter felt a stab of grief when she heard the Sun's reply.

"Your daughter has gone to the place from which no one returns," said the Sun. "Hades himself carried her off to the underworld to be his bride."

Demeter's sorrow was great. She wandered the earth, month after month, grieving. And while Demeter mourned, no crops grew. Winter winds blew over the land. The fields turned hard and cold. Trees shed their leaves, and grapevines bore no fruit. The people starved.

Winter lasted many long months. All over the world, men and women prayed to Demeter to bring back the spring, the crops, the green earth. But Demeter was too sad to hear them.

Finally, the king of the gods, Zeus, decided that he must do something. He sent his messenger, Hermes, to see Hades in the underworld.

The moment that Hermes arrived in the world of the dead, Persephone grew cheerful for the first time. "You've come to take me back," she sighed. "I know it!"

Hermes spoke to Hades. "Dread ruler of the dead, I come from your king, Zeus. The world above is dying. You must give up your bride."

Hades did not want to let her go. But when Zeus commanded, the other gods had to obey. However, Hades had a plan. He knew that once a mortal had eaten in the underworld, she could never leave. Until now, Persephone, in her grief, had touched no food. So Hades spoke to his bride.

"Well," he said in a kind voice, "you get your wish. You may return to your mother. But, before you leave me, let us taste food together."

"The world above is dying," said Hermes.
"You must give up your bride."

With that, Hades offered her a fruit called a pomegranate. Persephone did not know that she would bind herself to the world of the dead forever. She ate one seed before she left.

At last, Persephone joined her mother. They rushed into each other's arms and wept with joy. Then, Demeter heard about the pomegranate seed. She knew there would still be trouble.

Later, when Demeter was called to appear before Zeus, she feared she might once again lose her daughter.

Hades, too, stood before Zeus. He claimed that since Persephone had eaten the seed, she must remain in the world of the dead forever. Demeter said that if she lost her daughter, the earth would never see springtime again.

At last, Zeus made his decision.

*When Persephone first returns, Demeter is so
happy that the world grows green and bright.*

"Hades," said Zeus, "you may have your bride beside you for four months of every year. From December until March, Persephone will sit beside you on the throne of death.

"But Demeter, for the other eight months of the year, your daughter will be yours. She will be free to live in the world of sunlight and laughter."

And that is why the seasons appear on the earth. When Persephone first returns from the land of the dead, Demeter is so happy that the world grows green and bright, lasting all through the summer months. Then, as winter nears, Demeter grows sad and fall begins. Finally, Persephone leaves her mother to join her dark husband. Demeter, in her grief, sends harsh winter on the world.

The Fastest Bride

"No! No! No!" shouted Atalanta. "No man will ever marry me! I'm faster, stronger, and smarter than any man alive. So why should I marry?"

Atalanta was right. She was the fastest human being on the face of the earth. She was a great huntress. No beast was too strong or too smart for

"I'm faster, stronger, and smarter than any man alive," said Atalanta.

her. She used her spear and sword to slay boars, lions—even dragons.

Atalanta was not only strong, she was also beautiful. Many men fell in love with her. But Atalanta would have nothing to do with any of them. And neither would her father.

There was a secret to Atalanta's strength and speed. She had been raised by a bear! Her father had wanted a son. He was so upset when Atalanta was born that he left the baby to die in the forest. But a mother bear found Atalanta and raised her as her own. Atalanta grew up strong and cunning among the animals. She knew the ways of the wild. She feared nothing.

She never learned who her father was until the day she entered a wrestling match. Her father, the king, had invited young men from miles around to wrestle. He wanted to see who was the strongest.

Many of the men were shocked when a woman said she wanted to enter the match. "Go back to your sewing," shouted one of the men. "A girl has no place at a wrestling match!"

"I'm not going to wrestle with a woman!" said another. "If I hurt her, I'd never forgive myself."

But Atalanta knew how to make them give in. "You are only saying that because you are cowards. You're afraid that you'll lose to a woman!"

That did it. Right away, the young men asked the king to let Atalanta enter the match.

The match began. For two days, Atalanta wrestled one man after another. Each fell before her great strength and speed. Before long, Atalanta was declared the winner.

At last, the king said, "The winner is Atalanta, the strongest man—I mean person—in the kingdom."

That night at the feast, Atalanta told her story about the bear who had raised her. The king knew at once that this amazing woman was the baby he had left to die. With tears in his eyes, he confessed to his daughter. Atalanta forgave him. Atalanta now had the family she had always wanted. And the king had a daughter who was stronger than any son could have been.

But soon, the problem of marriage arose. Young men showed up by the hundreds to ask for Atalanta's hand. They wanted her for a wife because she was strong and beautiful.

Atalanta, however, didn't want to get married. She was perfectly happy the way she was. But she soon grew tired of making excuses.

"He's too poor," she would say. Or, "He's too fat." Or, "He's too short."

Finally, after she had used every excuse she could think of, even more young men showed up at the palace. Atalanta's reputation had spread far and wide.

Then she came up with a plan. She told her father, and together they called a meeting of the young men.

"Atalanta has agreed to marry," announced the king. A great cheer went up among the young men. "On one condition," the king continued. The hall became very quiet. "Atalanta will marry the man who beats her in a foot race."

"*Atalanta has agreed to marry,*"
announced the king.

Now a groan went through the crowd. They knew that no man alive was faster than Atalanta. But that didn't stop them from trying.

They came singly and in groups. They came from all over the world. But time after time, race after race, Atalanta beat them all to the finish line. It looked as if Atalanta would remain single forever.

But on Mount Olympus, the home of the gods, there was one who didn't like the way Atalanta treated those young men. Aphrodite, the goddess of love, decided it was time for Atalanta to get married.

There was a certain young man who had often prayed to Aphrodite for help. His name was Melanion. Some of the young men prayed to Zeus or Apollo. But Melanion knew that he must pray to the goddess of love, for love was in his heart.

Aphrodite heard his prayers and decided to help him. One morning, after Melanion had prayed all night to the goddess, he awoke to find three golden apples beside him.

At first, he was so amazed at their beauty that he didn't stop to wonder where they had come from. Then he thought about his prayers to Aphrodite. He thought about the golden apples. At last, he understood what he must do.

Atalanta is fast and strong, he said to himself. *But I am clever. Against cleverness and the goddess of love, no one can win — not even Atalanta.*

That day, Melanion challenged Atalanta to a race.

"Good!" she said. "Another race. I love

to race. But most of all, I love to win!"

Melanion smiled to himself. Soon they stood at the starting line. The king gave the signal, and they were off.

In the beginning, Melanion was able to keep up with Atalanta. For almost a mile, they were even. Then Melanion could feel Atalanta edging ahead of him.

It's time for the first of the three apples, thought Melanion. He reached into his bag, took out one of the apples, and threw it ahead in their path. The apple rolled and came to a stop.

When Atalanta saw the apple, she couldn't believe her eyes. It was the most beautiful thing she had ever seen. It lay in the grass, glowing in the golden sunlight. She couldn't resist. She stopped to pick up the apple. As she did, Melanion pulled ahead.

Once again, Atalanta stopped.

For a short time, he kept the lead. But Atalanta deserved her reputation for speed. In a few moments, she had caught up with him. Once again, she began to pull ahead. Melanion dropped the second of his three golden apples.

Again, Atalanta's eyes were dazzled by the beauty of the apple. Once again, she stopped. And again, Melanion pulled ahead.

Now they were approaching the finish line. Melanion watched Atalanta speed past him. He watched the finish line draw near as Atalanta sped toward it.

I've got to throw it just right, he thought, *and Atalanta will be mine.*

When she was only a few feet from the finish line, Melanion threw his last golden apple. It was a perfect throw. It rolled in front of Atalanta and then off the track into the grass. Atalanta stopped to pick up the apple. Melanion sped across the finish line and won.

Later that day, Atalanta and Melanion were married. Melanion had his heart's desire. And Atalanta learned that Melanion's love was even stronger than she was.

Odysseus and the One-Eyed People Eater

Odysseus was a great Greek king. Of all the Greeks, Odysseus was the cleverest.

After he helped the Greeks defeat Troy in battle, he and his men got lost as they were sailing home. Soon, they were out of food and water. They thought they would starve to death until they saw an island.

"At last!" shouted the crew. "Food! Water! Land!"

Under the orders of Odysseus, they sailed to the island. When they landed, Odysseus took twelve of his best men and set out to explore the island. They took with them a jug of wine to trade for food.

Soon they found a large cave. Odysseus called out, "Hello! Is anybody there?" There was no reply, so they went inside.

To thirteen hungry men, that cave was the answer to all their prayers. Inside, they found whole roasted lambs, giant slabs of cheese, clusters of grapes, and figs. Odysseus and his men began to eat.

But their happiness did not last long. A huge shadow fell across the cave opening. The cave grew dark as a giant stepped inside. He had only one eye — one huge eye in the middle of his forehead. The giant herded his sheep into the cave. Then he closed off the opening with a giant rock.

The giant saw that some of his food was gone. "Who eats my food?" boomed the one-eyed giant.

Odysseus spoke up. "Lost travelers who seek help," he said. "We kindly ask to trade for food."

But the one-eyed giant only laughed. He quickly grabbed two of the men, one in each hand, and threw them against the wall of his cave. Then he roasted them in the fire and swallowed them whole.

The giant herded his sheep into the cave.

As he ate, the giant paid little attention to the rest of the human beings. After his meal, he lay down and began snoring loudly. Odysseus and his men huddled together in horror.

The next morning, the giant awoke and ate two more men for breakfast. He roasted them and swallowed them just like the first two. Then he took his sheep out to graze for the day. But before he left, he put back the large stone so the humans couldn't escape.

All day long, Odysseus racked his brain, thinking of a plan. At last, he had an idea and told his men what to do. At once, they took a large pole and sharpened one end of it with their swords.

As the sun was going down, the giant returned to his cave for the night. While Odysseus and his men watched, the one-eyed giant took two more of Odysseus's men and ate them for dinner.

After the giant had eaten, Odysseus spoke. "Would you like some wine after your dinner?" he asked.

"Wine? What is that?" asked the giant.

"It's a drink well loved by humans," said Odysseus.

With that, the giant grabbed the jug out of Odysseus's hands and drank it all in one gulp.

The giant grinned. He liked it. Soon, the wine began to take effect. The giant curled up by the fire and began to snore. Odysseus and his men sprang into action.

They put the sharpened end of the pole in the fire until it was smoking hot. It took all the men to lift it out of the fire. With Odysseus in charge, they took aim. Together, they rammed the sharp,

"Would you like some wine after your dinner?"
Odysseus asked.

burning point into the giant's eye.

The giant awoke with a howl that shook the cave. He pulled the burning stake out of his eye.

"I'm blind! I'm blind!" he roared in pain. He staggered around the cave trying to catch Odysseus and his men.

His giant hands found one of the men. In rage, the giant crushed the man into powder with his hands. But Odysseus knew that with the giant blinded, their chance of escaping was much better.

Soon, the giant grew tired from the wine and the wound, and again he fell asleep. Odysseus carried out the rest of his plan.

As the giant slept, Odysseus and his men tied the sheep together, side by side, in threes. Then, each man tied himself under the belly of the middle sheep. They waited there until morning.

At sunrise, the giant awoke and prepared to take his sheep out for the day. He rolled the stone back, and herded the sheep out. But as they went through the opening, the giant felt each sheep to make sure that the humans weren't escaping.

In his blindness, the giant was fooled. He couldn't tell that the sheep were tied together in threes. The giant inspected his sheep, but he never felt the bellies of the middle sheep. One by one, the men escaped.

At last, when they were all out of the cave, they cut themselves loose and ran for their ship. The giant heard their shouts and chased after them.

Luckily, the men were able to reach their ship. The giant heard the oars splashing in the water and threw large boulders into the sea. He took aim by listening to the sound of the oars. Finally, the ship was far enough away that the giant couldn't reach it.

"Who has done this to me?" the giant yelled at last. "I want to know who has come to my island and blinded me! What is your name?"

Odysseus, thinking quickly, answered the giant. "My name is 'Noman,'" said Odysseus. "Noman has done this to you."

"I'll get you for this, Noman!" shouted the giant, and at once, he went to the other giants for help.

"What's wrong?" they asked him. "Who has put out your eye?"

"Noman!" answered the giant. "Help me catch him!"

"What do you mean?" laughed the

The giant threw large boulders into the sea.

other giants. "How could no man put your eye out?"

"Stop laughing," demanded the giant, "and help me catch Noman!"

"How can we help you catch no man?" demanded the other giants, growing angry. The blinded giant grew angry, too, and soon all the giants were fighting with each other.

While the giants fought over Noman, Odysseus and his men sailed away to safety.

The King Who Turned to Stone

The Gorgons are three hideous monsters. They are sisters. They have wings, and, instead of hair, snakes grow on their heads. But the most terrible thing about the Gorgons is that anyone who looks at them turns to stone.

Only one man will ever face them and live—a young man named Perseus.

Perseus and his mother live on a little island ruled by a cruel and evil king, Polydectes. One day, Polydectes sees Perseus's mother.

I must have this beauty! Polydectes says to himself. Then he sees Perseus. *So, she has a son,* thinks Polydectes. *I'll get rid of him, and then do with his mother as I please.*

Polydectes returns to his palace and plans a way to get rid of Perseus. *I'll let the Gorgons take care of this little chore for me,* he thinks. He sets his plan in motion.

The next day, the king announces that he is about to be married, and he will give a feast. Perseus is startled to find that he has been invited to the wedding feast.

Perseus puts on his best clothes and walks to the palace. When he arrives, he finds that all the other guests have brought rich gifts for the king.

I have no money or rich gifts to bring, thinks Perseus. *All I have is my strength and courage.* Perseus doesn't know that he has fallen into the trap of Polydectes.

One by one, the guests present their gifts to the king. Then it is Perseus's turn. He rises and speaks before all the nobles in the hall.

"Great King Polydectes," Perseus begins in a loud voice. The hall grows quiet. "I am a poor man and have no fine gifts to bring. But I offer you a gift better than any here, for I offer the gift of courage. In honor of your marriage, I will kill Medusa, the Gorgon!"

"I offer you the gift of courage,"
Perseus told the king.

The hushed crowd breaks into a roar. "Who is this brave young man?" some ask. "Who is this foolish boy?" ask others. They all know that no one can kill Medusa. No one can get close enough. Just one look, and anyone who sees her is turned to stone.

Polydectes smiles to himself. Perseus has done exactly what the king hoped he would do.

Good, thinks Polydectes. *As soon as Perseus has turned to stone, his mother shall be my bride!*

Perseus leaves the hall in a daze. "What have I done?" he moans. "I'll never find Medusa. And even if I do find her, how will I ever kill her?"

Perseus does not know it, but he has a powerful friend to help him—Hermes, the messenger of the gods.

Perseus searches all over Greece hoping to find help. After many months, Hermes appears before him. Hermes wears winged sandals and a winged cap.

"I have come to help you, Perseus," says Hermes. "But before I help you find the Gorgons, you must prepare yourself well. You will need four things. First I will give you a magic sword. It will cut through anything in heaven or on earth.

"Next," says Hermes, "take this shield. You will need it on your quest."

Perseus looks at the shield. It is smooth and polished, and it shines like a mirror.

"You must not look at Medusa, or you will turn to stone," warns the god. "So use this shield as a mirror. Use its reflection to look at Medusa when you aim your sword.

"The third magic thing that you will need," says Hermes, "is the cap of invisibility. The cap makes anyone who wears it invisible. But the cap is not in my power to give. It is guarded by three old women who share one eye among them. I'll show you how to trick them into giving you the magic cap."

Hermes tells Perseus how to find the women who guard the cap and how to trick them out of it. Finally, Hermes gives Perseus his winged sandals.

"With these sandals," Hermes explains, "you can fly over air, earth, fire, and water."

For many days, Perseus flies over strange lands, searching for the three old women. At last, as evening falls, he spies them in a forest, sitting around a fire.

*For many days, Perseus flew over
strange lands.*

The three women have only one eye among them. One woman uses it for a while. Then she takes it out of its socket and hands it to another. Round and round they pass the eye, from socket to socket. Perseus watches as they take turns with it.

At last, one of the women takes the eye out of its socket and begins to hand it to another. At that moment, when none of them can see, Perseus leaps out and snatches the eye.

At first, each blind woman thinks that one of the others has the eye. But after a few minutes, they realize that none of them has it, and none can see.

"Who's there?" asks one of the blind women, afraid that someone has tricked them. "Who has taken our only eye?"

"Don't be afraid," says Perseus. "I

have taken your eye. And I will gladly give it back, if you give me the cap that makes its wearer invisible."

The three women argue with Perseus. "You have no right to take our eye!" one of them shouts. "The cap of invisibility is ours, and no one shall have it!" argues another. Then they begin to argue with each other. But, at last, they give in. After all, Perseus has their only eye, and they can't see without it. Angrily, they give the cap to Perseus.

Perseus is now prepared for his dangerous task. He has the sword and shield of Hermes, and the invisible cap from the three old women. He puts on his winged sandals and flies out across the sea, looking for the island of the Gorgons.

In the distance, he can see the island. Luckily, the three Gorgons are sleeping.

They are horrible creatures, three times larger than a man. They have giant wings and snaky hair.

Perseus puts on his cap and becomes invisible. He flies down over the island, and comes as close as he can without looking into Medusa's face.

As he draws nearer, Perseus looks into the shield to take aim. He hovers above Medusa and raises the magic sword, gazing at her reflection in the shield. *Swish.* He brings down the sword. The sharp edge slices through Medusa's scaly neck.

Keeping his eyes firmly fixed on the reflection in his shield, Perseus grabs the cut-off head by its snaky hair. He plunges the head into a sack.

Instantly, Medusa's sisters awake. They rise with a terrible, ear-piercing

*Medusa's sisters rose with a terrible
ear-piercing cry, and chased Perseus.*

cry, and chase Perseus. But because of the cap of invisibility, they cannot find him. Perseus escapes. The head of Medusa is safely in his sack.

When Perseus finally returns to his little island, he discovers new trouble. His mother has refused to marry Polydectes, and the king has sworn revenge. Now his mother is in hiding.

When Perseus hears what has happened to his mother, he decides to take care of the wicked king once and for all. He flies to the palace where Polydectes is holding another feast. Perseus steps into the hall. Suddenly, he removes the cap of invisibility.

The king and all his guests look up. "Who is this golden youth with a sword and shield worthy of the gods?" they wonder. "Who is this who appears out of thin air?" At last, Polydectes recognizes him.

"Well, Perseus," says Polydectes, "I knew you would be too cowardly to slay Medusa."

"You're wrong, King. I did kill her, and here's the proof!" All eyes are upon him now. Perseus reaches into the sack and pulls out the head of Medusa. He holds it out in front of him for all to see. The eyes of every person at the feast look at the hideous face.

All at once, a great cry goes up. The guests try to run, to turn their eyes away. But it is too late. They have begun to turn to stone. Their feet are rooted to the ground. Their bodies will not move. They watch in horror as flesh and blood turn into cold, lifeless stone before their eyes.

Moments later, what was once a feast is now a room full of statues. The king is frozen with a look of horror on his face.

With the king dead, peace returns to the small island. Perseus has won fame and fortune throughout the land as a great hero.

Pygmalion

Some said he was ugly. Some said his first love had rejected him. Others said he was extremely shy. Whatever the reason, the fact remained – Pygmalion hated women.

From his youth, when other boys walked in the fields with their sweethearts, or showed off in games and battles, Pygmalion remained indoors. He worked at the only thing he really loved. Pygmalion made statues. He was a sculptor.

As the sun peeped over the eastern hills, Pygmalion could be found hard at work in his room. Before him stood a large block of marble. Hour after hour, day after day, Pygmalion used his hammer and chisel to carve the hard stone.

Other boys grew into men, married, and had sons and daughters of their own. Pygmalion, on the other hand, stayed in his room and learned to breathe life into lifeless stone.

"Pygmalion," his friends would say, "why don't you come to the festival of Aphrodite with us? Maybe you'll find a woman who could love even you!"

"I'm busy," Pygmalion would always answer. "I have better things to do than

*Before Pygmalion stood a large
block of marble.*

waste my time with women."

After a while, his friends gave up. Soon, no one bothered Pygmalion. He began to work on the greatest statue of his life—the form of a beautiful woman.

For a year, Pygmalion worked on the woman in stone. For someone who hated women, it was strange for Pygmalion to try to create the perfect woman.

She was beautiful and graceful. The statue showed a nobility of mind and spirit. Every good human quality seemed to shine forth from her. Bit by bit, the stone fell away to reveal the form beneath.

After the year had passed, Pygmalion placed his chisel on the stone for the last time. He gently hammered away a small piece. Then Pygmalion stood back.

There, he thought. *She's finished.* He

stood for hours and stared with wonder at the beautiful statue he had created.

She's wonderful, he thought. *So beautiful and noble. So lifelike!*

It was true. The statue was perfect. The woman of stone looked real. Strangers passing by thought a woman of flesh and blood stood in the house of Pygmalion. They wondered why she didn't move. Only when they touched the stone could they believe she was a statue and not a real woman.

Soon, people came from miles around to stare in wonder at the magnificent statue. Pygmalion become jealous. He locked his door. He would let no one but himself admire her.

A strange thing began to happen. Pygmalion fell in love. He, who had cursed love, was now cursed by it. He

The woman of stone looked real.

brought her clothes, hoping they would please her. He brought her rich gifts – jewels and pets – hoping she would thank him. But she just stood as always – lifeless and cold.

Aphrodite, the goddess of love, pitied Pygmalion. She was moved by his strong passion and devotion. The goddess decided that if Pygmalion humbled himself before her, she would help him.

Soon, it was time for the festival of Aphrodite. Pygmalion had always refused to go. But this year, he felt differently. He had an urgent prayer in his heart for Aphrodite.

People arrived at the festival from near and far. They came to show thanks to Aphrodite for giving love to the world. Some came to ask for her help. Pygmalion traveled along with them.

He had a favor to ask, too.

At the festival, each person came before the altar of Aphrodite. One by one, they knelt before the flame and said a prayer. Pygmalion waited in line. His prayer burned in his heart.

At last, he knelt before the altar. Passionately, he prayed to the goddess of love.

"Aphrodite," he prayed, "show me kindness and mercy. I will serve you all my days if only you will help me find a woman like my statue!"

Suddenly, the flames on the altar shot up in a shower of sparks. Pygmalion and the crowd fell back in wonder and surprise. The flame shot up a second time, then a third. Pygmalion was happy. He knew Aphrodite had heard his prayer. He knew sooner or later Aphrodite would help him find a woman like his statue.

When Pygmalion arrived home, he saw his statue standing there. "Perhaps somewhere in the world," he said to the statue, "there is someone like you." He reached out and touched her arm. He jumped back.

Could it be? he thought. *Is it possible?* He touched her arm again. There was no doubt about it. She felt warm to his touch. He touched her again, and she was still warm.

Finally, he approached her. He took her in his arms and kissed her. At first, she felt lifeless. But slowly, he felt her breath rise to her lips. He kissed her again. And at last, she returned his kiss.

Pygmalion jumped back. He couldn't believe his eyes. Color spread over her face. She was blushing! Then her eyes

*Suddenly, the flames on the altar shot up
in a shower of sparks.*

fluttered open. She looked at Pygmalion and smiled.

Aphrodite had rewarded Pygmalion more than he had ever dared to hope. The statue had come to life! A beautiful woman of flesh and blood stood before him. The goddess had answered his prayer.

Pygmalion named her Galatea. Soon they were married. And Pygmalion loved and honored her the rest of his life.